PON

EEK!

Stories to make you shriek™

For Beginning Readers
Ages 6-8

This series of spooky stories has been created especially for beginning readers—children in first and second grades who are developing their reading skills.

How do these books help children learn to read?
- Kids love creepy stories and these stories are true page-turners (but never too scary).
- The sentences are short.
- The words are simple and repeated often in the story.
- The type is large with lots of room between words and lines.
- Full-color pictures on every page act as visual "clues" to help children figure out the words on the page.

Once children have read one story, they'll be asking for more!

For my island Dad—M.F.

For Maggie, my good friend and string enthusiast—J.D.

Text copyright © 1997 by Margaret Frith. Illustrations copyright © 1997 by Julie Durrell.
All rights reserved. Published by Grosset & Dunlap, Inc., a member of The Putnam &
Grosset Group, New York. EEK! STORIES TO MAKE YOU SHRIEK is a trademark of
The Putnam & Grosset Group. GROSSET & DUNLAP is a trademark of Grosset &
Dunlap, Inc. Published simultaneously in Canada. Printed in the U.S.A.

Library of Congress Cataloging-in-Publication Data

Frith, Margaret.
    Mermaid Island / Margaret Frith : illustrated by Julie Durrell.
    p. cm.—(Easy to read)   (Eek! Stories to make you shriek)
    Summary: Jane enjoys spending time on the beach with her new friend Molly, but Molly's
reluctance to go swimming may hide an interesting secret.
    [1. Mermaids—Fiction. 2. Beaches—Fiction.] I. Durrell, Julie. ill. II. Title. III. Series. IV.
Series: Eek! Stories to make you shriek.
    PZ7.F91865Mh 1997   97-19380
    [Fic]—dc21   CIP
    ISBN 0-448-41725-1 (GB)   A B C D E F G H I J   AC
    ISBN 0-448-41618-2 (pb)   A B C D E F G H I J

y-to-Read
es 6–8

EEK!

Stories to make you shriek™

Mermaid Island

By Margaret Frith
Illustrated by Julie Durrell

Grosset & Dunlap • New York

We are here!

On a little island

in the middle of nowhere.

My dad, my mom, and me.

My dad is a writer for <u>Getaway</u> magazine.

Every summer we get away to really cool places.

This time it is a really hot place.

Mermaid Island.

I picked it,

because I really like the name.

I wake up and look out of my window.

I see someone swimming.

It is a girl.

She has red hair.

She swims really fast.

She dives down.

Wow! Can she stay

underwater for a long time!

I run down to the beach.

I am too late.

I have missed her.

The next day I see her again.

She is swimming with someone.

Two red heads against a blue sea.

Maybe it is her mother.

I run down to the beach.

"Hello!" I shout.

But they are too far out

to hear me.

Later I see a man on the beach.

"Hello," I say. "I'm Jane.

Do you know the girl with red hair?

She swims here every morning."

He smiles. "That's my Molly.

The two of us live here all year.

I will tell her to come and see you."

"Great!" I say.

"We will be here all week."

That afternoon it is too hot

for the beach.

I am lying on the porch.

I hear someone coming.

I open my eyes.

Sea-green eyes stare at me.

"Hello. I'm Molly.

Dad said you were looking for me."

"Hi! I'm Jane.

I hoped you would come over."

Molly is wearing a T-shirt,

jeans, socks, and sneakers.

I wonder how she can stand

all those clothes in this heat.

"Want to go swimming?" I ask.

"Mmmm . . . I can't," Molly says.

"I've got a sunburn."

Well, that explains the jeans.

"Let's look for shells," she says.

"Great," I say. "I love shells.

I want to take some home."

We head down to the beach.

Molly is wearing a pretty shell

on a ribbon around her neck.

"I have never seen one like it," I say.

"It is called a whistler,"

Molly tells me.

"They are very hard to find."

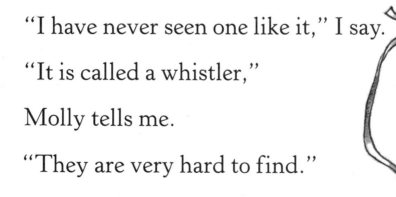

"Do you think I can find a whistler?"

"I don't know," Molly says.

"My mother gave me this one.

But she lives pretty far away.

So I don't get to see her much."

Funny. That lady swimming with Molly

had the same red hair.

"Wasn't that your mom . . ." I start to say.

But Molly looks away quickly.

"Ooh, Jane!" Molly says,

running along the beach.

"A lion's paw!"

I run after Molly.

I forget about her mother.

The next day Molly comes again.

It is just as hot.

And now she is wearing sweatpants.

"Hi," I say. "Feel like swimming?"

Molly shakes her head.

"Can't. My legs still hurt.

Let's build sandcastles."

So we do.

Molly is so good at it.

She shows me how to drip wet sand

through my fingers.

We make tall towers.

We dig tunnels and moats.

"It looks like a magical castle," I say.

Molly gets a dreamy look on her face.

"My mom took me to a castle

like this once."

We stay on the beach for hours.

We have so much fun.

The sun is going down.

I ask Molly if she

can spend the night.

"I'll go ask my dad."

Her dad says yes!

She comes over in time for supper.

We are having fish.

Molly looks at her plate.

She doesn't touch the fish.

"I'll just eat the other stuff,"

she tells my mom.

"I hope you don't mind."

Later we get ready for bed.

Molly takes a bath first.

She stays in the tub forever.

I hear splashing and singing.

Then it is my turn.

There is water everywhere.

And weird.

I see shiny pieces of something

in the tub.

I pick them up.

They look like silvery scales from a fish.

I like Molly a lot.

But is there something strange going on?

In the morning, it is raining.

Molly asks me over to her house.

Her bedroom is cool.

All the walls are painted

to look like the sea.

Even the ceiling.

It is like being underwater.

I feel as if I am swimming

in a school of fish.

I love it!

We spend the day painting.

Molly's pictures are wonderful.

And different.

She paints all kinds of fish

I have never seen before.

And mermaids swimming

around underwater islands.

"Oh, Molly. Your paintings look so real.

Just like out of a movie."

Molly gives me one to keep.

She is a really special friend.

The week is going by so fast.

It stops raining.

But the sun doesn't come out.

I don't care.

Every day Molly has something new

for us to do.

We explore a cave.

We go out in a glass-bottomed boat
with her dad.

She shows me a waterfall.

Finally the sun comes out again.

It is the day before we go home.

And I am sad.

"Today I want to show you

my favorite place," says Molly.

We go along a cliff.

Up a steep hill.

The ocean is all around us.

"This is my lookout place,"

Molly tells me.

"What do you look out for?"

I ask.

Before she can answer,

I hear a big splash.

I look down and see a huge fish tail

dive into the waves.

"What was that?" I ask Molly.

"Mmmm . . . I'm not sure. . . .

Maybe a dolphin," she says.

I don't say anything.

It did not look like a dolphin to me.

Its tail was silvery and shiny.

And I saw a flash of red hair.

Like Molly's.

At least I think I did.

But maybe it was seaweed.

The next day—my last day—

I go down to the beach very early.

Molly is going to meet me here.

The waves are very big today.

Soon Molly comes. And surprise!

She is wearing a bathing suit.

She has a towel around her,

like a long skirt.

"Jane, this week has been so much fun.

I wish you lived here too."

Molly bites her lip.

"I want to show you something."

She sounds a little scared.

"What, Molly?" I ask.

She takes off her towel.

I can't believe it.

Molly's legs are all silvery

and they have scales—

like a fish!

I just stare.

"What-what happened to you?"

I say at last.

Molly takes my hand.

"I will tell you," she says.

"But let's go swimming first.

My mother is coming to meet us.

Then you will understand."

We dive into the waves.

The water feels great!

I swim way out with Molly.

The waves are big and strong.

I start to get tired.

I try to swim back.

But the waves carry me

out farther.

I am getting scared now.

"Molly, help!"

Molly swims back to me.

She holds me up and

tries to swim to shore.

She is strong.

But not strong enough.

We are getting nowhere.

A wave hits me in the face.

I swallow water and sputter.

I am struggling.

Molly looks scared.

"Hold on, Jane," she says.

"My mother will help us."

She takes her whistler and blows.

A high whistle flies over the waves.

A second later Molly shouts,

"She's coming!

My mother is coming!"

Something is swimming toward us.

Fast.

I feel arms catch hold of me.

I am carried over the waves.

Soon I feel the sandy bottom

under my feet.

I am safe.

I look into sea-green eyes like Molly's.

"Thank you," I say.

She smiles and turns toward the sea.

I watch red hair and a shiny tail

dive through a wave.

Now I understand about Molly.

Her mother is a mermaid!

She swims to Molly.

They both wave to me.

"Come back next year!"

Molly calls out.

I nod my head and smile.

"I will!"

I'm home now.

Today a package arrives from

Mermaid Island.

It is from Molly.

Inside is a whistler.

Dad says that it is a very rare shell.

It is found deep down on the ocean floor.

"I wonder where Molly got it," Dad says.

I don't.